I Can Ride My Bike

By Julie Ellis

Illustrated by Melissa Webb

Luka's new bike was blue and red.

Luka liked his new bike.

He got on it.

Wobble, wobble, **CRASH!**

Luka fell off his new bike.

"I will help you ride your bike on Saturday," said Dad.

They put the bike away in the shed.

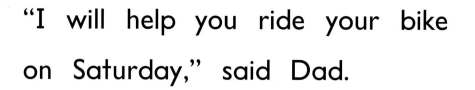

Luka looked at his new bike.

He wanted to ride it now.

Saturday was three days away.

Luka got his bike

out of the shed.

Luka got on his bike.

"I **can** ride my bike," he said.

Then Luka saw the tree.

Wobble, wobble, **CRASH!**

Luka fell off his bike.

Luka's sister Tara came out.

"I want to ride my bike,"
Luka said to Tara.

"I will help you," she said.

Tara helped Luka get on his bike.

"I **can** ride my bike," said Luka.
Then Luka saw the puddle.

Wobble, wobble, CRASH!

Luka fell off his bike.

Luka's mom came out.

"I want to ride my bike," said Luka.

"I will help you," said Mom.

Mom helped Luka get on his bike.

"Look," said Mom.

"You can stop the bike like this."

Luka got on his bike again.

This time he stopped.

He did not fall off.

"I **can** ride my bike!" said Luka.

On Saturday, Luka said to Dad,
"I **can** ride my bike."
Then he saw the dog.

Wobble, wobble, STOP!

"Did you see me, Dad?
I can ride my bike,"
said Luka.
"I can **stop** my bike, too!"